Now One Foot,
Now the Other

Story and Pictures by
Tomie dePaola

G. P. Putnam's Sons
New York

For Bob

Library of Congress Cataloging-in-Publication Data
dePaola, Tomie. Now one foot, now the other. Summary: When
his grandfather suffers a stroke, Bobby teaches
him to walk, just as his grandfather once taught him.
[1. Grandfathers–Fiction.] I. Title PZ7.D439 No. [E] 80-22239
ISBN 0-399-20774-0 (HC)
20
ISBN 0-399-22400-9 (PBK)
25 27 29 31 30 28 26 24

Bobby was named after his best friend, his grandfather, Bob. When Bobby was just a baby, his grandfather told everyone, "Bobby will be three years old before he can say Grandpa, so I'm going to have him call me Bob."

And "Bob" was the first word Bobby said.

Bob was the one who helped Bobby learn to walk.

"Hold on to my hands, Bobby," his grandfather said. "Now one foot, now the other."

One of the best things Bob and Bobby did was to play with the old wooden blocks that were kept on a shelf, in the small sewing room under the front stairs.

The blocks had letters on two sides, numbers on two sides and pictures of animals and other things on the last two sides. Bob and Bobby would slowly, very slowly put the blocks one on top of the other, building a tall tower. There were thirty blocks.

Sometimes the tower would fall down
when only half the blocks were piled up.

Sometimes the tower would be almost finished.

"Just one more block," Bob would say.

"And that's the elephant block," Bobby would say.

And they would carefully put the elephant block on the very top.

But Bob would sneeze and the tower would fall down. Bobby would laugh and laugh.

"Elephants always make you sneeze, Bob," Bobby would say.

"We'll just have to try the next time," his grandfather would say.

Then Bob would sit Bobby on his knee
and tell him stories.

"Bob, tell me the story about how you
taught me to walk," Bobby would say.

And his grandfather would tell Bobby
how he held Bobby's hands and said,
"Now one foot, now the other. And before
you knew it . . ."

On Bobby's fifth birthday, Bob and he had a special day. They went to the amusement park. They rode a roller coaster, ate hot dogs and ice cream. They had their pictures taken in a machine, and they sang a song and made a phonograph record.

And when it got dark, they watched the fireworks.

On the way home, Bob told Bobby stories.

"Now, tell me the story about how you taught me to walk," Bobby said.

And Bob did.

Not long after Bobby's birthday, his grandfather got very sick. Bobby came home and his grandfather wasn't there.

"Bob is in the hospital," Dad told Bobby. "He's had what is called a *stroke*."

"I want to go see him," Bobby said.

"You can't, honey," Mom told him. "Right now Bob's too sick to see anyone. He can't move his arms and legs, and he can't talk. The doctor's not sure if he knows who anyone is. We'll just have to wait and hope Bob gets better."

Bobby didn't know what to do. He didn't want to eat; he had a hard time going to sleep at night. Bob just *had* to get better.

Months and months and months went by. Bob was still in the hospital. Bobby missed his grandfather.

One day when Bobby came home from school, his father told him that Bob was coming home.

"Now, Bobby," Dad said, "Bob is still very sick. He can't move or talk. When he sees your mother and me, he still doesn't know who we are, and the doctor doesn't think he'll get any better. So, don't be scared if he doesn't remember you."

But Bobby *was* scared. His grandfather *didn't* remember him. He just lay in bed.

And when Dad carried him, Bob sat in a chair. But he didn't talk or even move.

One day, Bob tried to say something to Bobby, but the sound that came out was awful. Bobby ran out of the room.

"Bob sounded like a monster!" Bobby cried.

"He can't help it, Bobby," Mom said.

So, Bobby went back to the room where Bob was sitting. It looked like a tear was coming down Bob's face.

"I didn't mean to run away, Bob. I was scared. I'm sorry," Bobby said. "Do you know who I am?"

Bobby thought he saw Bob blink his eye.

"Mom, Mom," Bobby called. "Bob knows who I am."

"Oh, Bobby," Mom said. "You're just going to upset yourself. Your grandfather doesn't recognize any of us."

But Bobby knew better. He ran to the small sewing room, under the front stairs. He took the blocks off the shelf and ran back to where Bob was sitting.

Bob's mouth made a small smile.

Bobby began to build the tower.

Halfway . . .
Almost to the top . . .
Only one block left.

"OK, Bob," said Bobby. "Now the elephant block." And Bob made a strange noise that sounded like a sneeze.

The blocks fell down and Bob smiled and moved his fingers up and down.

Bobby laughed and laughed. Now he knew that Bob would get better.

And Bob did. Slowly, he began to talk a little. It sounded strange but he could say "Bobby" just as clear as day. Bob began to move his fingers and then his hands. Bobby still helped to feed his grandfather, but one day Bob could almost hold a spoon by himself. But, he still couldn't walk.

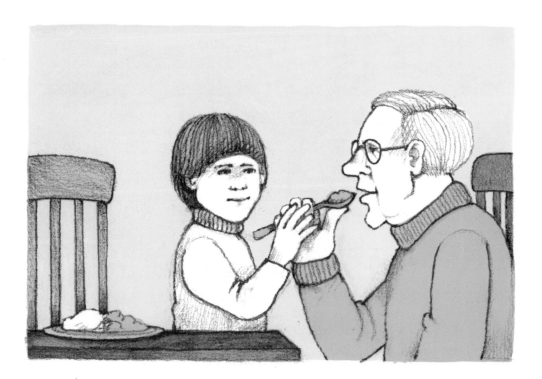

When the weather got nice and warm, Dad carried Bob out to a chair set up on the lawn. Bobby sat with him.

"Bobby," Bob said. "Story." So, Bobby told Bob some stories.

Then, Bob stood up very slowly.

"You. Me. Walk," said Bob.

Bobby knew exactly what Bob wanted to do.

Bobby stood in front of Bob and let Bob lean on his shoulders.

"OK, Bob. Now one foot."

Bob moved one foot.

"Now the other foot."

Bob moved the other.

By the end of the summer, Bob and Bobby could walk to the end of the lawn and Bob could talk better and better each day.

On Bobby's sixth birthday, Bobby got the blocks. Slowly he built up the tower. Only one block to go.

"Here, elephant block," Bob said.

Bobby put it on top.

Bob sneezed!

"Elephants always make you sneeze, Bob," Bobby said. "We'll just have to try the next time. Now, tell me some stories."

Bob did.

Then Bob said, "Bobby, tell story how you teach Bob to walk."

"Well, Bob, you leaned on my shoulders and then I said, 'Now one foot, now the other.' And before you knew it . . .'"